W9-BFK-403

Hiya! My name Thudd. Best robot friend of Drewd. Thudd know lots of stuff. Why ocean is salty. How octopus change color. Why continents always moving.

Drewd like to invent stuff. Thudd help! Now Drewd help Uncle Al make new underwater invention. Oop! Accident happen! Adventure happen! Want to come along? Look for giant squid? Turn page, please!

Get lost with
Andrew, Judy, and Thudd
in all their exciting adventures!

Andrew Lost on the Dog
Andrew Lost in the Bathroom
Andrew Lost in the Kitchen
Andrew Lost in the Garden
Andrew Lost Under Water
Andrew Lost in the Whale

AND COMING SOON!
Andrew Lost on the Reef

ANDREW LOST

6

IN THE WHALE

BY J. C. GREENBURG

ILLUSTRATED
BY MIKE REED

A STEPPING STONE BOOK™

Random House 🏠 New York

*To Dan and Zack and Dad
and the real Andrew, with love.
And to Jim Thomas, Mallory Loehr,
and all my Random House friends,
with an ocean of thanks.*
—J.C.G.

To Jane, Alex, and Joe.
—M.R.

Text copyright © 2003 by J. C. Greenburg. Illustrations copyright © 2003 by Mike Reed. All rights reserved under International and Pan-American Copyright Conventions. Published in the United States by Random House Children's Books, a division of Random House, Inc., New York, and simultaneously in Canada by Random House of Canada Limited, Toronto.

www.randomhouse.com/kids
www.AndrewLost.com

Library of Congress Cataloging-in-Publication Data
Greenburg, J. C. (Judith C.)
In the whale / by J. C. Greenburg ; illustrated by Mike Reed. — 1st ed.
   p.   cm. — (Andrew Lost ; 6)
"A stepping stone book."
SUMMARY: While trying to recover from their accidental underwater adventure, Andrew, his cousin Judy, and Thudd the robot are swallowed by a blue whale, the world's largest creature.
ISBN 0-375-82524-X (trade) — ISBN 0-375-92524-4 (lib. bdg.)
[1. Blue whale—Fiction. 2. Whales—Fiction. 3. Cousins—Fiction.]
I. Reed, Mike, ill. II. Title. III. Series: Greenburg, J. C. (Judith C.).
Andrew lost ; 6.
PZ7.G82785 Ir 2003   [Fic]—dc21   2003002662

Printed in the United States of America
First Edition 10 9 8

RANDOM HOUSE and colophon are registered trademarks and A STEPPING STONE BOOK and colophon are trademarks of Random House, Inc. ANDREW LOST is a trademark of J. C. Greenburg.

CONTENTS

ANDREW'S WORLD

Andrew Dubble

Andrew is ten years old, but he's been inventing things since he was four. Some of his inventions have gotten him into trouble, like the time he shrunk himself, his cousin Judy, and his little silver robot Thudd down to microscopic size with the Atom Sucker.

Andrew is in hot water again. He fooled around with his Uncle Al's underwater vehicle, the Water Bug. Now Andrew, Judy, and Thudd are about to be eaten by a whale!

Judy Dubble

Judy is Andrew's thirteen-year-old cousin. She thought she was too smart to let Andrew drag her into another crazy adventure. But that was before he showed her the Water Bug. . . . Now she's busy trying to save giant squids!

Thudd

The **H**andy **U**ltra-**D**igital **D**etective. Thudd is a super-smart robot and Andrew's best friend. Thudd must never get wet. If he does, his thought chips could get soggy. But Andrew, Judy, and Thudd had to go outside the Water Bug to fix it. Will Thudd stay dry?

Uncle Al

Andrew and Judy's uncle is a top-secret scientist. He invented Thudd and the Water Bug. Uncle Al is worried about Andrew, Judy, and Thudd. He's finishing up a new underwater vehicle called the See Horse so that he can rescue them!

The Water Bug

It used to be an old Volkswagen Beetle until Uncle Al turned it into a submarine. Andrew, Judy, and Thudd are pretty safe when they're inside it. Too bad they had to get out . . .

Soggy Bob Sloggins

This bad guy of the sea is building Animal Universe, the biggest theme park in the world. But Soggy Bob doesn't care about the animals. He hung a sign above the aquarium in Squid World. It says SOGGY BOB'S GIANT SQUIDWICHES—COMING SOON!

Now Soggy Bob is after Andrew, Judy, and Thudd, too. Will they be able to stop Soggy Bob from turning giant squids into giant snacks? Or will Soggy Bob get them into the biggest Dubble trouble ever?

A WHALE OF A PROBLEM

"YOWZERS!" yelled Andrew as he floated under the shadowy green water. His eyes bugged out. Something that looked like a blue-gray submarine was swimming toward him and his cousin Judy. Its mouth was as big as a garage!

Swarms of pink shrimp creatures swirled around them. The monster mouth swooped closer.

"Cheese Louise!" yelled Judy. "It's coming right at us!"

Her eyes were wide behind the face mask

of her Bubble Duds underwater suit.

meep . . . "Blue whale!" came a squeaky voice from a pocket of Andrew's Bubble Duds. It was Andrew's little silver robot friend, Thudd.

meep . . . "Blue whale big, big, big!" said Thudd. "Big as six brontosaurs! Big as twenty-five elephants! Long as three school buses!"

Ooooooooaaaaaaaaaaaauuu! came a huge sound through the special headphones in the helmet of Andrew's Bubble Duds. The Bubble Duds headphones picked up every sound, even some that humans couldn't usually hear.

Andrew could feel the sound, too. It shook him from his head to his toes.

Judy dove under the Water Bug. The Water Bug was an underwater vehicle made from an old Volkswagen Beetle.

"Andrew!" yelled Judy. "Get back into the Water Bug right now. That whale is going to *eat* us!"

meep . . . "Drewd and Oody too big for blue whale to eat," said Thudd. "Blue whale eat tiny shrimpy stuff."

Thudd pointed to the little pink creatures all around them. "Called krill," said Thudd.

Andrew dove under the Water Bug. He tried to find the button to get them back inside. But the gigantic mouth and its blubbery lips were just inches away!

"Noooo!" yelled Judy.

"Holy moly!" yelled Andrew.

"Noooop!" squeaked Thudd.

The mouth swooshed up a swimming pool–sized gulp of water—and Andrew, Judy, Thudd, and the Water Bug with it!

Just like that, they were inside the biggest mouth in the world. The rushing water tumbled and tossed them toward the darkness at the back.

Andrew whammed into something bouncy as a trampoline.

meep . . . "Whale tongue!" said Thudd.

"Wowzers!" said Andrew. "It looks like a big gray sofa pillow, but it's longer than my living room!"

meep . . . "Blue whale tongue weigh more than hippopotamus!" said Thudd.

Andrew clung to the side of the tongue

and looked around. Judy had disappeared!
And he couldn't see the Water Bug anywhere.
He tried to pull himself toward the front of
the mouth, but water kept pouring in and
pushing him back.

"Judy!" he yelled.

"Up here, Bug-Brain!" came Judy's voice.

BAD TIME FOR A BOOBY

Andrew looked up. Around the edge of the whale's mouth, in the place where teeth would be, were rows of black fringes. They were as long as a person's leg and hung down like a curtain all around the whale's mouth. Judy was clinging to a piece of the fringes.

"It's like I landed in some disgusting car wash," she said.

meep . . . "Oody hanging on baleen," said Thudd. "Made from same stuff as fingernails. Whale scoop up millions, millions of krill. Squash water out of mouth with tongue. Krill get stuck in baleen. Tongue scoop krill from baleen."

"Then I'd better get off this stupid stuff before I get squashed and swallowed, too!" Judy said.

She let go of the baleen and swam down to the tongue next to Andrew.

"Hey!" she said, pointing below the tongue. "There's something shiny down there. It's got to be the Water Bug!"

"Super-duper pooper-scooper!" said Andrew. "Let's get it and get out of here!"

Just then a clump of seaweed smacked into Andrew. As he tugged it off, he accidentally pulled open the pocket with Thudd in it!

The little Bubble Bag that kept Thudd dry flipped out.

"Thudd!" cried Andrew.

"What's the matter?" asked Judy.

"Thudd fell out of my pocket!" Andrew said.

Andrew squinted through the rushing water. All he could see was little pink krill. But then something large and shaggy and white swirled past.

It couldn't be a bird, thought Andrew. *Could it?*

But it was! It looked like a seagull with big red webbed feet and a long blue beak. And caught in its beak was Thudd.

Andrew reached out for the bird and snagged a big red foot!

"Thudd!" yelled Andrew.

Andrew wedged himself between the whale's tongue and lip. Then he tugged the Bubble Bag, with Thudd inside, from the bird's beak. Andrew tucked Thudd back into the pocket of his Bubble Duds.

meep . . . "Booby bird grab Bubble Bag," said Thudd.

"It really is a silly-looking bird," said Judy.

"But it's not nice to make fun of it," said Andrew, still holding on to the bird. "It saved Thudd."

meep . . . "Not make fun!" said Thudd. "Bird name is red-footed booby. Fishing bird. Booby hold breath and dive to catch fish. Whale catch booby! Booby catch Thudd!"

The rush of water slowed. It was getting darker. The gigantic mouth was closing!

Judy quickly snapped on Andrew's mini-flashlight.

Andrew felt a sharp tapping on his arm. The booby was pecking him. The bird cocked its head and looked up at him, then blinked its beady black eyes.

meep . . . "Drewd and Oody breathe cuz of Bubble Duds," said Thudd. "Booby not hold breath much longer!"

"Uh-oh," said Andrew. "We have to do something fast. Judy, hang on to him. I need to check my pockets."

Judy slipped the flashlight into a pocket of her Bubble Duds and grabbed the booby.

Tat! Tat! Tat! The booby was pecking at Judy's face mask.

"Knock it off, booby!" she said.

Andrew reached into a front pocket. Nothing there. He tried another pocket and found something squishy. It was a patch for the Bubble Duds, in case the underwater suit got torn.

"Perfect!" Andrew said. He stretched the patch over the booby's head and wrapped it firmly around the bird's neck. There was just enough to make a helmet for the booby. Just its beak was sticking out.

The bumpy green Bubble Duds material had bubbles of oxygen in it and pulled oxygen out of the water, too. Now the booby could breathe.

"*Gack!*" squawked the booby.

Judy handed the booby back to Andrew.

As the whale's mouth closed, the baleen from the top of the mouth slipped below the whale's bottom lip. It was dark as night, except for the beam of light shining up from the flashlight in Judy's pocket.

Suddenly the giant tongue pushed up! The roof of the giant mouth was only inches above them!

meep . . . "Hide under tongue!" said Thudd.

Andrew and Judy slid below the tongue. Andrew felt the baleen brushing the top of his head. It was stiff and plasticky.

SSSHHHHHHHHHHHHHH . . .

The humongous tongue was squishing water out through the baleen! Andrew, Judy, and the booby were squashed against the side of the whale's mouth.

In a few seconds, all the water was gone. Andrew and Judy were left smooshed against the baleen and covered with krill.

"I feel something sucking," cried Judy.

"Me too!" yelled Andrew.

The sucking started at Andrew's feet, then pulled at his legs, then dragged at his whole body. It was like the whale's mouth was a vacuum cleaner and he was a dust bunny.

"Yikes!" hollered Judy. "We're getting swallowed!"

GULP!

The beam of the flashlight narrowed to a thin thread as Judy disappeared down the whale's throat.

"Errrgggh!" yelled Andrew as his legs were pulled into the throat. It felt like the tightest rubber band was wrapping itself around him.

"Gack! Gack! Gack!" cried the booby.

Andrew held the booby over his head to keep it from being squashed. The throat squeezed and tugged and dragged Andrew down and down. It was like getting swallowed by a giant snake!

meep . . . "Muscles in throat take us to whale stomachs!" said Thudd.

Andrew could barely breathe. He felt a pile of krill plop down on his head.

THUMPA THUMPA THUMPA came a muffled drum-like sound.

meep . . . "Hear heart of whale beating?" asked Thudd. "Heart is big as Water Bug!"

Ploorp!

It was the sound of Judy plopping out of the throat.

"Yeeeuuuw!" came Judy's voice from below.

For the first time, Andrew was glad to hear Judy say "Yeeeuuuw!" It meant she wasn't totally squashed!

Ploorp!

Andrew and the booby landed next to Judy in a heap of krill.

"Whew!" said Andrew, taking a big breath. "At least there's room to breathe."

"*Gack!*" The booby hopped out of Andrew's

arms. It shook out its feathers, stretched its wings, and gobbled up a beakful of krill.

"Pee-yew!" said Judy. "What a stinky place!"

meep . . . "First stomach of whale!" said Thudd. "Whale got three stomachs."

Andrew grabbed the flashlight and flicked it around. They were in a closet-sized sack. Its yellowish walls were wavy and folded. There were some pebbles at the bottom, near Andrew's feet.

The walls of the sack started to ripple.

Bluuuuuurf!

Piles of krill poured down from the whale's throat over Andrew and Judy. The booby fluttered out of the way.

"Gross-a-mundo!" said Judy, wiping krill off her face mask. "And I'm allergic to seafood. I think I'm getting hives from these things!"

She started scratching her arms through her Bubble Duds.

"You'd better not do that," said Andrew.

"You'll make it worse. Wow! Look at all this junk the whale swallowed."

Sticking out of the pile of krill were a tire, a tin can, bottles, a bunch of silver birthday balloons tied with red ribbons, and a rubber duck.

Judy looked up to the top of the stomach.

"Maybe we can get out the way we came in," she said. "Like Santa Claus." She pointed to where the throat connected with the stomach. It looked like the opening of a dark chimney.

The rippling walls of the stomach began moving in and out!

"Uh-oh!" said Andrew.

"Cheese Louise!" yelled Judy.

It felt like a giant hand was squeezing the stomach.

"Gack! Gack!"

The booby flapped its wings nervously. Andrew wrapped his arms around it to calm it down.

meep . . . "Whale not got teeth to smoosh food," said Thudd. "But whale got three stomachs. First stomach smoosh food. Little stones and pebbles help to smoosh."

Thudd pointed to the booby. "Bird not got teeth, either. Bird eat little stones, too."

The stomach gave a sudden squoosh that tumbled Andrew off his feet and into the smooshy krill goo.

"Help!" yelled Judy.

When Andrew sat up, he saw the top half of Judy sticking out of an opening in the stomach wall.

Andrew set the booby on a small pile of krill and handed Judy the flashlight. Then he grabbed her arms and tried to pull her back. But the stomach was stronger than Andrew. Judy's shoulders, then her head, disappeared into the hole.

The stomach lurched and Andrew flopped backward. Before he could get up, his feet got pulled into the hole!

Ooofers! thought Andrew. *It feels like I'm getting squeezed through a drinking straw!*

Andrew reached for the booby and held it above his head again to protect it.

After a minute of squishing, *ploorp!*— Andrew plopped through the hole.

"Welcome to the purple palace!" said Judy.

By the beam of the flashlight, Andrew saw he had landed in a purple sack. This stomach was bigger than the one they'd just come from. The walls were wrinkly—and they were squirming!

meep . . . "Second stomach!" said Thudd.

Bluuuuuurf!

Pink piles of krill started pouring in.

Judy's face looked green through her face mask.

"This is the *worst!*" she said, wiping pink slime off her Bubble Duds.

Then something juicy started to ooze from the walls and slowly fill the stomach.

meep . . . "Stomach make acid to digest food," said Thudd. "Break food into mole-cules! Bubble Duds protect Drewd and Oody from acid."

"*Gack!*" said the booby.

It looked at Andrew and blinked.

"Uh-oh," said Andrew. "There's not enough Bubble Duds for the bottom of the booby!"

STOMACH PROBLEMS

The stomach started churning like a washing machine. The stomach acid was sloshing.

Judy managed to reach into her pockets and pull out a Bubble Duds patch.

"This isn't big enough to help," she said.

Just then a stomach rumble tossed Judy into a slimy pink heap.

"*Ick!*" she yelled.

As she kicked her way out, her foot got tangled in the bunch of silver birthday balloons. She pulled them off. One of the balloons was ripped. She untied its ribbon and tossed the balloon to Andrew.

"Here," said Judy. "Wrap the booby in this. These balloons are bad for sea animals. Dolphins and birds and seals can choke if they swallow them. But maybe this time a balloon can *help* a bird.

"You can use the ribbon to tie the balloon on the booby," Judy continued. "But don't let him eat it."

Andrew got tossed against the wall of the stomach. It felt like it was made out of bicycle tire. He braced himself against the stomach and stuffed the booby into the torn balloon. He tied it around the bird's foot with the ribbon.

As the stomach acid swirled around the stomach, the krill got mushier. Andrew, Judy, and the booby didn't!

Suddenly the purple button in the middle of Thudd's chest started to blink. Andrew and Judy's Uncle Al, the man who'd invented

Thudd and the Water Bug, was about to visit them by hologram.

Thudd's purple button popped open and a see-through purple hologram of Uncle Al zoomed out.

Andrew and Judy were tossing like underwear in the wash. Uncle Al's smiling face seemed to bounce all over the purplish stomach.

"Hey there, guys!" said Uncle Al.

"Hi, Uncle Al!" said Andrew and Judy.

"Hiya, Unkie!" said Thudd.

"I've been having a hard time reaching you," said Uncle Al. "You sound a little, um, blubbery."

With his hologram, Uncle Al could hear them but couldn't see them.

"That's because we're inside a whale's stomach!" said Judy, sloshing back and forth.

meep . . . "Blue whale!" said Thudd.

Uncle Al's fuzzy eyebrows poked up

toward his shaggy hair. "Queen Isabella on a jelly doughnut!" he said. "You're inside the biggest animal that ever lived! I hope you're wearing the Bubble Duds."

"We've got the Bubble Duds on," said Andrew. "They're really comfortable!"

"That's good," said Uncle Al. "Stomach acid can dissolve almost anything eventually. Even metal!

"The Bubble Duds will protect you, but only for two hours. Then they could start to, uh, come apart."

"Cheese Louise!" said Judy. "How do we get out of here? Could we get the whale to throw up or something?"

"Which stomach are you in?" asked Uncle Al.

"The second one," said Andrew.

"Hmm," said Uncle Al. "The whale can't throw you up from the second stomach. It looks like you'll have to take the long way out. You've got one more stomach to go—"

"Oh, brother!" Judy interrupted. "Another stupid stomach."

Uncle Al smiled. "You know that cows have four stomachs," he said.

"So what?" said Judy.

"Well," said Uncle Al, "whales are related to cows and some other animals with hooves. Fifty million years ago, the ancestors of whales lived on land. They looked kind of like hairy crocodiles and they had little hooves on their toes!"

"Bizarre-o!" said Judy.

"Yup," said Uncle Al. "But let's get back to the most important thing—getting you home safely. Where's the Water Bug?"

"It's under the whale's tongue," said Andrew.

"Ah!" said Uncle Al. "Then the Water Bug must be caught in the whale's gigantic mouth pouch!"

Judy mashed her fist into a little island of krill floating in the soupy mess.

"Tough tomatoes!" she said. "Does that mean we'll have to go back into the whale's mouth?"

"I'm afraid so," said Uncle Al. "And when you get back to the Water Bug, set the destination dial for Hawai'i and come back immediately."

Andrew and Judy looked at each other. Their whale of a problem had started in Hawai'i. That's where Andrew had accidentally set the Water Bug on a search to find a giant squid. But the giant squids were in danger from a bad guy named Soggy Bob Sloggins. He wanted to capture some for his theme park!

Andrew hesitated. "Um, first we've got to save the giant squids from Soggy Bob," he said.

Uncle Al frowned and shook his head.

"I was afraid of that," he said. "I've been working on a new underwater vehicle, the See Horse. My plan is to catch up with you and help you. But the See Horse isn't finished yet."

"So meanwhile," said Judy, "we're going to get pooped out by a whale!"

Uncle Al nodded. "You need to get pooped out as fast as you can," he said. "Remember, the Bubble Duds could start to fall apart after two hours."

Uncle Al's hologram began to wobble.

"Uncle Al!" yelled Judy. "You're jiggling."

"Listen, guys," said Uncle Al. His voice was shaky. "I could disappear any minute. But I'll keep trying to—"

The Uncle Al hologram made a sound like popcorn popping. Then it disappeared.

The stomach was scrunching Andrew and Judy harder and harder. It started to shove them through another tiny opening in the stomach wall.

BLUFFOOOWEEEE!

Andrew struggled through the hole with the booby.

Ploorp!

He splashed down into a dark space. Wetness squished around him. *I wish I had my flashlight,* he thought.

"*Gack!*" said the booby.

Andrew patted the booby's head.

"Yerrrgh!" came Judy's voice in the darkness. "I'm stuck! It feels like I'm being squeezed through a keyhole!"

"Um, try to push," said Andrew. "Do you

want me to pull your head or something?"

"No way, Bug-Brain!" said Judy.

She grunted and struggled.

"Okay, okay," she sighed. "When I count to three, you pull my head and I'll push."

Andrew put down the booby, felt around for Judy's head, and grabbed it.

"One . . . two . . . three!" said Judy.

Andrew yanked, Judy shoved, and finally—

Ploorp!

Judy ended up in the third stomach, too.

As she poked the flashlight through the darkness, they saw they had landed in a place that looked like the inside of a green balloon. Sticky yellow-green goo was squirting out from a hose-like opening on one side of it.

meep . . . "More juice to digest stuff," said Thudd. "From liver."

Bluuuuuurf!

A river of pink mush poured in from

the second stomach. It didn't look like krill anymore.

"What time is it, Thudd?" asked Judy.

meep . . . "Two o'clock," said Thudd.

"So we have to get out of this whale before four o'clock," said Judy. "Before our Bubble Duds start to fall apart and we turn into whale chow."

THUMPA THUMPA THUMPA

They were closer to the whale's heart.

There was another, quieter sound, too.

thumpa thumpa thumpa

"It sounds like the whale has two hearts!" said Andrew.

"Maybe it's an echo," said Judy.

meep . . . "Not echo," said Thudd. "Sound echo off of hard stuff. Rocks. Metal. Whale made out of soft stuff. Whale not got two hearts, either. Big whale got baby whale inside."

"Wow!" said Judy.

"Jumping gerbils!" said Andrew.

The last stomach gave them one more squirt of liver juice. Then it started to squeeze them out into something that seemed like a tight pink stocking. Andrew went in head-first, holding the booby in front of him. It was slippery inside, and fuzzy, too, like a towel.

The pink tube squeezed and tugged. It was like being inside a boa constrictor.

"Yuck-a-rama!" said Judy.

meep . . . "Intestines!" said Thudd. "This part is small intestine. Fuzzy stuff pull food molecules into blood."

Judy groaned. "There's only one thing that interests me about intestines. *Getting out of them!* It could take hours for the intestines to shove us out. We've got to get out fast! *Move it, Andrew!*"

"Woofers!" said Andrew, crawling along and pushing the booby ahead of him. "It's so hot and stinky in here."

meep . . . "Whales got warm blood, like humans," said Thudd. "Whales got same temperature as humans. That why whale got lots of blubber fat. Keep whale warm in cold water. Like fur keep polar bear warm in cold air. Lotsa years ago, people hunt whales for blubber. Melt blubber fat. Make oil. Use oil to burn in lamps. Make candles, soap, lotsa stuff."

Spluuurt!

Slimy juices were squirting out of the intestine.

"Gack! Gack!" said the booby. Andrew could feel it trying to flap its wings.

"It's okay, little buddy," he said. "We'll get out soon—I hope."

Judy passed the flashlight up to Andrew as they shoved their way through the goo.

meep . . . "Whale intestine five hundred feet long," said Thudd. "Almost long as two football fields. Human intestine thirteen feet long."

A soft rumble came up behind them.

FFFLOOOOOOOOF!

A big puff of wind, like air bursting out of a balloon, blew past them.

"Pee-*YEW!*" said Judy. "That was un-believably stinky!"

meep . . . "Lotsa little bacteria eat stuff in intestine," said Thudd.

"Yum!" said Judy.

meep . . . "Then bacteria burp up stinky gas. Gas move through intestine. Make big noise!"

Andrew chuckled. "We know what *that* is!" he said. "It's a f—"

"Andrew!" yelled Judy. "Don't be disgusting!"

"*Gack! Gack!*" said the booby excitedly.

"What is it, little buddy?" asked Andrew.

The glow from the flashlight lit up a long white ribbony shape attached to the whale's intestine.

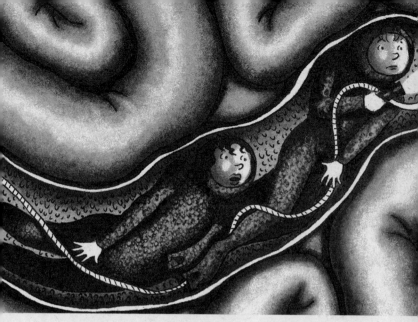

meep . . . "Tapeworm!" said Thudd. "One hundred feet long. Stick to intestine. Tapeworm soak up food juice through skin."

The booby cocked its head, opened its beak, and lunged toward the tapeworm.

meep . . . "Not eat!" said Thudd. "Tapeworm got lotsa eggs inside. Booby swallow eggs, get tapeworm, too!"

Andrew clamped his hand over the booby's beak.

"No tapeworm for you, buddy," he said.

Andrew and Judy tried to creep quickly past the tangled ribbon of tapeworm.

The intestine got wider.

meep . . . "Leave small intestine," said Thudd. "Large intestine ahead."

Pop! Pop! Pop!

The sounds were coming from the sleeves of Andrew's Bubble Duds. Some of the bubbles were bursting!

Pop!

A bubble on the booby's helmet burst, too!

"I hear your Bubble Duds popping," said Judy. "Mine are, too! What time is it?"

meep . . . "3:45," said Thudd.

"Uh-oh," said Andrew.

Andrew and Judy pushed on through the intestines.

Soon they found themselves in a larger space. It was piled high with reddish chunks the size of footballs.

"I guess we know what that is," said Andrew.

meep . . . "Whale poop!" said Thudd. "This is rectum. Poop collect here."

"It's disgusting," Judy said. "But it means there's a way to get out of here."

Before Judy could find what she was looking for, the rectum began to tremble. Then it gave a big squeeze!

Bluffoooweeee!

HEADS AND TAILS

Andrew, Judy, Thudd, and the booby blasted out of the rear of the whale!

"We're whale poop!" shouted Andrew.

Above them was the whale's huge gray tail. It was as wide as a street!

Judy tucked the flashlight into a pocket of her Bubble Duds.

"Catch that tail!" she said. "If we let the whale get away, we'll never get back to the Water Bug!"

As Andrew reached for the monster tail, he could see the rays of the sun slanting through the water.

meep . . . "Whale coming up to breathe," said Thudd. "Blue whale can stay underwater forty minutes. Some whales can stay underwater two hours!"

The whale's tail was just inches from Andrew and Judy. As it flapped down, it twirled the water into whirlpools that pushed the kids away.

meep . . . "Tails of whales and dolphins move up and down," said Thudd. "Tails of fish move side to side."

"Zip it, Thudd!" yelled Judy. "Andrew! Grab that tail!"

Andrew reached for it, but the tail was smooth and rubbery. It slipped away from his fingers.

meep . . . "Grab tip of tail!" said Thudd. "Got barnacles growing on it. Little animals in shells. Help to get grip on tail."

Judy managed to latch on to one of the pointy tips. The roughness of the barnacle shells helped her hang on.

Andrew grabbed Judy's foot with one hand and hung on to the booby with the other.

Andrew and Judy clung to the tail with all their might. In two flaps, the whale's tail crashed through the surface of the water!

"Wowzers schnauzers!" said Andrew.

"Yay!" said Judy. "It's so great to see the sun again."

PROOOOOOOOSH!

Far ahead, at the front of the whale, a huge fountain of mist rose into the air. It was

as high as a three-story building!

meep . . . "Whale breathe out old air," said Thudd. "Whale breathe with spout on top of head. Like nose!"

"We can get to the whale's mouth by going over its back," said Andrew.

Andrew and Judy dragged themselves onto the top of the whale's tail. They slithered along on their bellies. It was like creeping across a huge, slippery beach ball. They scrambled onto the whale's back.

Andrew paused for a moment. He pulled the Bubble Duds helmet off the booby and untied the ribbon that kept the balloon wrapped around the booby's body.

"Goodbye, booby!" said Andrew.

"*Gack!*" screeched the booby. It hopped onto the whale's back and stretched its wings. Then it hopped on Andrew's shoulder.

Andrew pulled down the helmet of his Bubble Duds. The sun felt warm on his face.

A cool breeze ruffled his hair. Judy pulled her helmet down, too.

"Gack! Gack!" said the booby. It lightly pecked Andrew's nose.

meep . . . "Booby say 'Thunkoo!'" said Thudd.

The booby flapped its wings and flew off.

Judy waved. "We'll miss you!" she yelled after it.

PROOOOOOOOSH!

The whale spouted again.

"Yeeuuuw!" said Judy. "A really bad case of fish breath!"

They crept toward the front of the whale. The whale's smooth blue-gray skin was marked with dark spots, like huge gray freckles.

Judy reached the whale's spout first.

There were two openings that looked like gray nostrils. They were as high as Judy's knees.

"It's a gigantic nose!" she said.

Judy looked in. "These nostrils are so big, babies could crawl into them!"

"Look!" said Andrew, pointing to a big lump inside the right side of the whale's

mouth. "It must be the Water Bug!"

"But the whale's mouth is closed," said Judy. "We can't get in."

meep . . . "Maybe whale eat again," said Thudd.

"Let's get closer to the front," said Judy. She tugged her helmet down over her face.

Andrew pulled his helmet down, too. They crept beyond the whale's spout.

The whale's head tipped to the side. Andrew and Judy began to slide down the side of the head!

OPEN WIDE!

Judy and Andrew slid past the whale's eye. It was dark brown and the size of an orange.

Judy waved. "I wonder if it can see us," she said. "I hope it can."

The whale's mouth was opening! Andrew and Judy grabbed on to the baleen and jumped down into the rushing water filling the mouth.

"Under the tongue!" yelled Andrew.

He and Judy plunged below. It was dark. Judy pulled the mini-flashlight out of her pocket.

"There's the Water Bug!" she shouted, and dove under it. Andrew followed.

He found the seat buttons and pressed them.

FLAMP!

The front seats of the Water Bug flipped out.

"Strap yourself in," said Andrew. "And press the button on the side of your seat."

FLAMP!

The seats flipped inside.

glurp . . . "Welcome back," said the mechanical voice of the Water Bug. "You were gone a long time. My computer said you would not return. What would you like to do now?"

"Start Escape Jet!" Andrew shouted.

The hood of the Water Bug clicked open and a fat black tube popped out.

Andrew pulled up on the steering wheel, looked over his shoulder, and slammed his

foot down on the gas pedal.

Slooooooosh!

The Water Bug jetted backward above the whale's tongue and past its rubbery gray lips. They were out!

Andrew switched off the Escape Jet and went back to regular power. The Water Bug's paddle wheels whizzed them through the water. Judy and Andrew tugged the Bubble Duds helmets off their heads.

"Wowzers schnauzers!" said Andrew. "We made it!"

Judy sighed. "I never thought I'd say this, but it's good to be back in the Water Bug! Let's follow the whale for a little while. She's beautiful. I have a feeling she likes us."

Thudd opened his Bubble Bag, crept out of Andrew's pocket, and hopped onto the dashboard.

The whale slowed down and rolled from side to side.

kk . . . kkk . . . kkkkk crackled the speaker on the dashboard.

"Well, ah'll be an oyster's auntie!" came a familiar growly voice from the speaker. "Them little water brats took a lickin' from the biggest blue whale ah ever did see. And they're still kickin'!"

"Oh no!" said Judy. "It's Soggy Bob!"

There was a flash of shiny metal underneath the whale. It was Soggy Bob's Crab-Mobile!

Its silvery claws and legs were tucked close to its body. Inside the glass dome at the top of the Crab-Mobile, Soggy Bob was sitting in his huge, zebra-striped chair. His bald head gleamed like a bowling ball. His skinny black mustache curled above his crooked smile.

Perched on the back of the chair was Bob's enormous blue parrot, Burpp, whose name was short for **Bob's Ultra-Robot Parrot Partner.**"

Awwk! screeched Burpp.

Clack! Clack! Clack! The Crab-Mobile's giant metal claws snapped in front of the Water Bug's windshield.

Soggy Bob grinned and twisted his

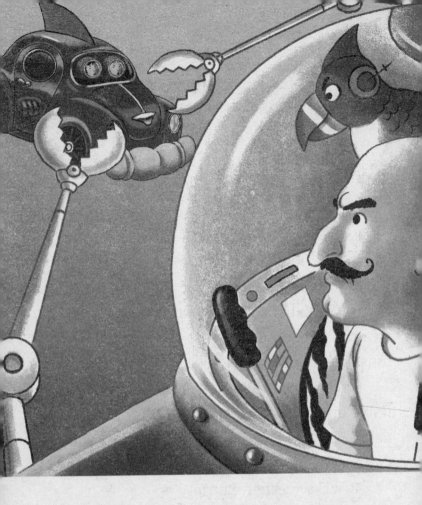

mustache. "What's your hurry, little mud puppies? You're just in time for the biggest show in the sea!"

BIG, BIG BABY!

"Look!" said Andrew, pointing past the Crab-Mobile. "The whale has two tails!"

Beneath the giant tail of the blue whale was a much smaller tail.

meep . . . "Mother whale having baby whale!" said Thudd. "Whale calf."

Quickly, the rest of the baby whale slid out.

"That's one super-sized baby!" said Judy.

meep . . . "Blue whale baby long as elephant!" said Thudd. "Weigh as much as forty humans!"

The mother whale circled and dove beneath the baby.

meep . . . "Mother whale push baby whale to top of water to breathe," said Thudd. "If baby whale not breathe soon, it drown!"

kk . . . kkk . . . kkkkk "And now, my little sardines," said Soggy Bob, "ya get to see me make my biggest catch! Yee-ha!"

The Crab-Mobile headed toward the baby whale. A lasso shot from one of its claws and looped around the tail of the baby! Soggy Bob pulled a lever in the Crab-Mobile. The lasso tightened. The calf was caught before its mother could get it to the surface! The Crab-Mobile was towing the baby away!

The mother whale swam after her calf. She tried to push the little whale up with the front of her head. But the Crab-Mobile was dragging it under!

"Don't do this, Mr. Sloggins!" yelled Andrew as he followed the calf. "The baby whale needs to breathe!"

"Ah see your little lips movin'," said Soggy Bob, "but ah can't hear a thing ya say. And that's the way ah like it!"

Andrew steered the Water Bug closer to the baby whale.

"Scat, ya little toads!" said Soggy Bob, shaking his fist. "Ya better stay away from my fish if ya know what's good for ya!"

Judy frowned. "He doesn't even know that a whale isn't a fish!"

"Maybe he doesn't know that whales need to breathe," said Andrew.

Andrew pressed the Octo-Tool button. The hood of the Water Bug popped open and the Octo-Tool's eight long tentacles wriggled out.

"Remove rope from baby whale!" Andrew commanded.

glurp . . . "Good idea," said the Water Bug.

The tentacles darted toward the rope, grabbed it, and untied it!

"Grrrr!" growled Soggy Bob. "That little whale critter is *mine*!"

Clack! Clack! Clack!

The claws of the Crab-Mobile snapped at the tentacles of the Octo-Tool. But the Octo-Tool was too quick. It whipped the lasso away from the Crab-Mobile.

"Rope Crab-Mobile claws!" yelled Andrew.

The Octo-Tool hurled the lasso around one of the Crab-Mobile's clunky claws and yanked it closed.

"Way to go!" cheered Judy.

"Drat!" yelled Soggy Bob. "Ya little water rats are askin' for big trouble!"

The Crab-Mobile's free claw snapped at the Octo-Tool.

The Octo-Tool roped that claw, too! Then the tentacles gave the rope a big jerk. The Crab-Mobile started to spin! It began to sink!

"Gotcha!" shouted Andrew.

"Double drat!" screamed Soggy Bob.

Andrew and Judy watched him madly yanking big metal handles inside the Crab-Mobile. Burpp flapped his wings and twisted dials with his beak.

But the Crab-Mobile kept spinning down and down.

"Ah'll be back!" yelled Soggy Bob,

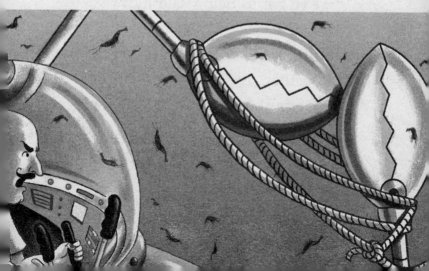

slamming his fists on the arms of his huge chair. "Ah'll be back faster than ya monkeys can eat a peanut butter sandwich!" He pushed his face against the glass dome and smiled a crooked smile. "And ah'll be servin' giant *squidwiches* soon! Heh heh heh!"

The Crab-Mobile sank out of sight.

"Good job!" said Andrew.

"Thank you," said the Water Bug.

"Look!" said Judy, staring at the baby whale. "It's struggling."

The mother whale was trying to push her calf up, but it kept slipping down into the water!

"We've got to help," said Judy.

Andrew drove the Water Bug close to one side of the calf. The mother was on the other side. Together, the mother whale and the Water Bug pushed the baby to the top!

They could see the spray as the little whale got her first breath of air through her blowhole! Then she dove under the belly of her mother to look for milk.

meep . . . "Baby blue whale gain eight pounds every hour," said Thudd.

Judy thought for a moment. "That's almost two hundred pounds a day!" she said. "That's the size of a big person!"

The blue whale and her baby pulled ahead of the Water Bug. Soon they were just dark shadows in the distance.

"They're so beautiful!" sighed Judy.

"I'll bet it will take Soggy Bob a while to untangle the Crab-Mobile," said Andrew. "The whales will be far away by then. They'll be safe. We'd better get back to saving the giant squids. If we don't get those lava boogers out of the Super-Sniffer, we won't be able to track them."

The Super-Sniffer was a gadget that could track anything in the water. Andrew and Judy needed it to find the giant squids. But it had gotten clogged with lava boogers!

"Yeah," said Judy. She thought for a minute. "It'll be easier to get the boogers out if we're above the water."

Andrew pulled the steering wheel up. The Water Bug popped to the surface. The sun was shining and feathery clouds drifted in the blue sky.

"Super-duper pooper-scooper!" said Andrew.

"Let's open the windows and get some air," said Judy.

Andrew pressed a button on the door and the side windows popped open.

"Yikes!" yelled Judy.

A thin silvery fish had flown right through her window. It landed in Andrew's lap.

ZAP!

meep . . . "Flying fish!" said Thudd.

Andrew gently picked up the flapping fish and slipped it out the window.

"Look at *these* weird things," he said.

The Water Bug was surrounded by transparent blue lumps the size of basketballs.

"Looks like a bunch of weird party balloons," said Judy.

"Noop! Noop! Noop!" said Thudd. "Jellyfish! Poison jellyfish. Called man-of-war. Got stinging tentacles! Hundred feet long! Big sting! Jellyfish not just one animal. Made up of lotsa little ones. Jellyfish like neighbor-hood. Some neighbors sting food. Some neighbors eat food. Some neighbors make baby jellyfish!"

Andrew scratched his head. "We'll have to go somewhere else to fix the Super-Sniffer," he said. "But right now I'm starving. Getting swallowed by a whale sure makes you hungry."

"Me too!" said Judy.

"I wonder what there is to eat around here," said Andrew.

He unbuckled his seat belt and leaned over his seat. Instead of having rear seats, the back of the Water Bug had a tiny kitchen with a refrigerator, a microwave oven, a sink, and a cabinet.

Andrew opened the refrigerator. Inside were piles of pizzas wrapped in plastic!

"Neato mosquito!" said Andrew. "We've got Uncle Al's special pizzas!"

As Andrew unwrapped a pizza, a white bird flew up from the water in front of the Water Bug. Big red feet slammed down on the hood of the Water Bug and walked up to the windshield.

"It's the booby!" yelled Andrew.

Thwack! Thwack!

It was pecking at the glass.

"I think it misses us," said Judy.

The booby pecked at the window again, flew off, and dove underwater.

meep . . . "Booby hunt for flying-fish eggs!" said Thudd.

"I'll stick with pizza," said Andrew, looking to see what kind it was.

As always, the crust was bright green. Uncle Al made crusts that glowed in the dark. The pizza was covered with Uncle Al's super-lumpy tomato sauce, lots of different cheeses, and a pile of onions.

Uh-oh, thought Andrew. *Onions. Yuck.*

He pulled off all the onions and stuck them in a pocket. Then he put the pizza into the microwave oven and set the timer for two minutes.

By the time Andrew pulled the hot slices from the oven, the sun had disappeared. Puffy white clouds were being chased by black cloud mountains.

Thudd pointed to the sky.

meep . . . "Storm clouds," he said. "White clouds made of tiny drops of water. Storm clouds made of big drops of water. Big drops make storm clouds look black."

Andrew handed Judy a slice of pizza. "We'll be safe in the Water Bug," he said.

As they munched, the sky turned dark as a dirty sock. Fat drops of rain smacked the windshield. They closed the windows.

A strong wind pushed the Water Bug along the waves, which were as high as a table. In minutes, they were as high as a

refrigerator, then high as a ceiling, then high as a house! Then higher! Andrew stopped chewing his pizza crust.

As the Water Bug rode to the tops of the waves, long white fingers of foam poked at the windows. Then the Water Bug zoomed down the insides of the waves like a roller-coaster car.

Suddenly zigzag fingers of lightning sizzled through the sky and crashed into the water.

CRRRRAAAACKKKKK! came a bang of thunder.

meep . . . "Water make electricity," said Thudd. "Little water molecules rub against each other. Electricity make lightning. Hotter than sun! Make air explode! Thunder happen! See lightning first cuz light go fast, fast, fast! Sound go slow! Light travel million times faster than sound!"

"Let's dive!" yelled Judy. "You're never supposed to be in a high place when there's lightning. The Water Bug sticks out above the water."

Before Andrew could pull down the steering wheel, his skin began to tingle. His hair stood straight out from his head!

A flash of dazzling white light surrounded the Water Bug! It was so bright that Andrew had to close his eyes. It was so bright that he could see everything in the Water Bug through his closed eyelids!

WHO'S HUNTING WHO?

Lightning had struck the Water Bug!

CRRRRAAAACKKKKK! came the thunder.

When Andrew opened his eyes, the Water Bug was sliding down to the bottom of a wave.

Judy's face was white as the moon. Her hair was standing out from her head like a frizzy clown wig. Her mouth was open and a piece of mozzarella cheese hung over her lip.

"Smokey the Bear!" she said. "We were almost toast!"

meep . . . "Water Bug protect Drewd and

Oody from lightning," said Thudd. "Electricity go through metal, not through Drewd and Oody!"

Andrew checked the Water Bug. The paint on the hood had bubbled up in a few places. It looked like the Water Bug had pimples. But everything else seemed okay.

"Let's get out of here!" said Judy. "NOW!"

Andrew pushed the steering wheel down. The Water Bug dipped under the waves.

"We'll hang out below until the storm passes," said Andrew. "Maybe we'll even find a quiet place on the ocean floor to get the lava boogers out."

Down and down they went through the dark green water. Strands of brown seaweed swirled by the windows.

As Andrew steered the Water Bug deeper and deeper, it got darker and darker. Andrew turned on the headlights.

"Look at all that weird white stuff in the

lights!" said Judy. "It's like we're in a snow globe!"

meep . . . "Sea snow," said Thudd. "Tiny animals, pieces of dead stuff, pieces of poop fall to bottom of ocean. Little fish eat sea snow."

"Gross!" said Judy.

At the end of the beam of the headlights, Andrew glimpsed a tall, dark shape.

"Wowzers!" he said. "Could that be an underwater skyscraper?"

"There's no sky to scrape down here, Bug-Brain!" said Judy.

As the Water Bug got closer, they could see the thing was a big tangle of pipes and pillars. It rose up through the water as far as they could see.

meep . . . "Oil rig!" said Thudd. "Bring oil from deep, deep hole under ocean. Oil happen when dead stuff get buried under lotsa rock. Millions, millions of years, dead stuff

HOW OIL FORMS

Dead stuff collects on the bottom of the ocean.

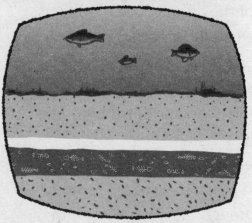

Dead stuff gets covered by layers of rock. Heat and pressure turn dead stuff into oil.

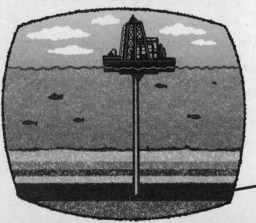

Oil companies drill through rocks to get the oil.

— oil layer

turn into oil! Burn oil to heat house. Gasoline made from oil."

"You mean we fill our gas tanks with things that lived millions of years ago?" said Judy.

"Yoop! Yoop! Yoop!" said Thudd.

"Weird!" said Judy. "Everything gets recycled!"

Andrew dove to find where the pipes sank into the ocean floor.

Judy pointed to a dome tucked close to the pipes. "What's that?" she asked.

Andrew slowly drove closer.

In front of the dome was a sign in big black letters:

Soggy Bob's Oil Rig and

Private Clubhouse

KEEP OUT!

"I don't believe it!" said Judy. "In the whole monster ocean, we keep running into Soggy Bob!"

Inside the dome, Andrew and Judy could see the Crab-Mobile—and Soggy Bob! He was tugging tangled ropes off the Crab-Mobile's claws. Burpp pulled at the ropes with his beak.

Soggy Bob turned when he saw the Water Bug's lights. He stomped up to the glass door and shook his fist. His thin eyebrows rose high on his bald head and his lips were moving fast. Andrew and Judy couldn't hear what he was saying, but they could tell it wasn't nice.

"Let's get out of here before he fixes that thing!" said Judy.

Soggy Bob's Oil Rig and Private Clubhouse KEEP OUT!

Andrew nodded. He pulled the steering wheel up and slammed the gas pedal to the floor. The Water Bug zoomed into the inky water.

Suddenly the headlights lit up a gray wall right in front of them.

Andrew was going too fast to stop. But just as they were about to crash, the wall swam away!

In the headlights, Andrew saw that the wall was really the side of a whale!

meep . . . "Sperm whale!" said Thudd.

"That's the whale in the Moby-Dick story," said Andrew. "Look what a huge head it has!"

meep . . . "Biggest head of any animal!" said Thudd. "Bigger than minivan! Head filled with tons of oil called spermaceti. Help whale dive deep, deep, deep! Sperm whale hold breath for hour!"

Judy frowned. "Sperm whales used to get hunted for the oil in their heads," she said. "People used to make perfume out of it!"

meep . . . "Sperm whale hunt giant squid!" said Thudd. "Sperm whale and giant squid have big battle in deep ocean!"

"Wowzers!" said Andrew. "If we follow that whale, maybe we'll find the giant squid!"

The whale sped through the water ahead of the Water Bug. Andrew tried to keep up. Outside, the blackness was turning green. Instead of leading them into the deep, the whale was swimming into shallower water. A strange landscape came into view—craggy hills sprouting blue antlers, gray brains, lacy yellow fans, and tall red feathers.

Suddenly Andrew and Judy slammed forward in their seats.

"Oofers!" said Andrew.

"Yeow!" said Judy.

"Eek!" said Thudd.

The Water Bug was flipping over and over!

When the Water Bug finally came to a stop, they were upside down! When Andrew's

head stopped spinning, he could see they were trapped in a huge web—a giant net!

Uh-oh, he thought. *We're looking for the giant squid, but I wonder what's looking for us. . . ."*

TO BE CONTINUED IN ANDREW, JUDY, AND THUDD'S NEXT EXCITING ADVENTURE!

ANDREW LOST ON THE REEF!

In stores April 2004

TRUE STUFF

Thudd wanted to tell you more about whales and other ocean creatures, but traveling through three whale stomachs and a lot of intestines tired him out! Here's what Thudd wanted to say:

• All mammals have hair. Some have a lot and some have just a little. Blue whales have hairs around their mouths. These hairs help them feel when krill are near. That way the whales know when to open their mouths!

• Blue whales make sounds that are very low. That means the vibrations that make up the sound travel very slowly. (You can see vibrations. Stretch an elastic band between your fingers, pull it gently, and let it go.) Humans can't hear very low sounds without special equipment.

Even though we can't hear them, the voices of blue whales are the loudest sounds made by any animal. Blue whales can communicate with each other from a thousand miles away! Only very low sounds could travel so far underwater.

• The ancestors of whales and dolphins are called Mesonychids (mez-ON-ih-kidz). These hairy creatures were about the size of large wolves. Fifty million years ago, they lived on land and hunted in the sea. Over time their bodies changed. Their nostrils moved up to the tops of their heads. Their legs and tails became flipper-shaped. And they lost most of their hair.

• Red-footed boobies can fly more than 3,000 miles over the ocean to hunt for food. The word *booby* comes from the Spanish word *bobo,* which means "clown." Spanish explorers thought the birds looked silly.

• Have you ever walked into a place that smelled really bad or really good? Did you notice that, after a while, the smell seemed much less smelly? Your nose was still sending the same smell messages to your brain, but after a while, your brain just doesn't pay much attention.

• During a storm, you can tell how far away lightning is. Count the seconds from the time you see lightning to the time you hear thunder. Divide the number of seconds by five to find how many miles away the lightning is. You will always see lightning before you hear the explosion it makes (thunder). That's because light travels a million times faster than sound.

Find out more!

Visit www.AndrewLost.com

WHERE TO FIND MORE TRUE STUFF

Want to find out about the amazing and mysterious things that can happen in the underwater world? Read these books! .

• *Eyewitness: Ocean* by Miranda Macquitty (New York: DK Publishing, 2000). Lots of information and great pictures tell the story of the oceans—how they were made, what lives in them, and how we explore them.

• *Oceans* by Seymour Simon (New York: HarperCollins Children's Books, 1997). You'll feel the waves when you see these pictures! Lots of great information, too. For example, there's 100 billion gallons of water in the ocean for each person on earth!

• *Lightning* by Seymour Simon (New York:

Mulberry Books, 1999) and *Storms* by Seymour Simon (New York: Mulberry Books, 1992). You'll know what's happening the next time the sky turns gray and boomy!

• *Sea Jellies: Rainbows in the Sea* by Elizabeth Tayntor Gowell (London: Franklin Watts, 1993). Jellyfish aren't fish. They don't have hearts or brains or bones, but they hunt and eat and reproduce. They can be smaller than your fingernail or bigger than a washing machine. You can find out how these blobby creatures live and see lots of them in this book.

Look at the next page
for a sneak peek at
Andrew, Judy, and Thudd's
next exciting adventure—

ANDREW LOST
ON THE REEF!

Available April 2004

1 TRAPPED!

Now I know what it feels like to be a fish! thought Andrew Dubble.

That was because Andrew's underwater vehicle, the Water Bug, was tangled in a huge net at the bottom of the ocean.

On the other side of the net were craggy mountains of coral and fish that looked like slices of a rainbow.

"Cheese Louise!" said Andrew's thirteen-year-old cousin, Judy. She was sitting next to Andrew in the passenger seat. "Maybe Soggy Bob set a trap to keep us from getting to the giant squids first!"

meep . . . "Try Octo-Tool," came a squeaky

voice. It was Andrew's little silver robot and best friend, Thudd. He was sitting in a pocket of Andrew's underwater suit.

"Good idea, Thudd," said Andrew.

He pressed a black button on the dashboard.

"Untangle Water Bug," said Andrew into a microphone near the steering wheel.

glurp . . . "Will try," came the voice of the Water Bug.

The hood of the Water Bug popped open and the gray tentacles of the Octo-Tool slithered out. They snatched at the net and tugged.

But the Water Bug wasn't coming free. Instead, the Octo-Tool's tentacles got tangled in the net, too!

glurp . . . "Alert! Alert!" said the Water Bug. "Octo-Tool trouble. Tentacles trapped!"

"Uh-oh," said Andrew. "Looks like we'll have to get out and do it ourselves."

Judy groaned. "Cheese Louise! The last time we left the Water Bug, we got swallowed by a whale!"

Andrew wasn't listening to her. "While we're out there," he said, "we can get the lava boogers out of the Super-Sniffer."

"Look!" said Andrew. He pointed to a part of the net ahead of them. It was squirming. "Something else is caught in the net."

meep . . . "Lotsa animals get caught in old fishing net," said Thudd. "Seals. Turtles. Dolphins."

Judy's eyes got wide. "You mean a dolphin could be trapped in there?" she said.

"Yoop! Yoop! Yoop!" said Thudd.

Judy sighed. "We've got to get out there right away and see what it is."

Judy and Andrew pulled their Bubble Duds helmets over their heads. Andrew made sure Thudd's Bubble Bag was tightly closed. Then Andrew sealed Thudd inside a front pocket of his Bubble Duds.

Andrew and Judy pressed buttons on the sides of their seats.

FLAMP!

Their seats flipped over, and they popped outside the Water Bug.

Andrew and Judy swam over to the squirming bundle in the tangled net.

Suddenly Judy stopped.

"Wait a minute," she said. "What if it's a shark?"

A STEPPING STONE BOOK™

Great stories by great authors . . . for fantastic first reading experiences!

Grades 1–3

FICTION
Duz Shedd series
  by Marjorie Weinman Sharmat
Junie B. Jones series by Barbara Park
Magic Tree House® series
  by Mary Pope Osborne
Marvin Redpost series by Louis Sachar
Mole and Shrew books
  by Jackie French Koller
Tooter Tales books by Jerry Spinelli

The Chalk Box Kid
  by Clyde Robert Bulla
The Paint Brush Kid
  by Clyde Robert Bulla
White Bird by Clyde Robert Bulla

NONFICTION
Magic Tree House® Research Guid
  by Will Osborne and
  Mary Pope Osborne

Grades 2–4

A to Z Mysteries® series by Ron Roy
Aliens for . . . books
  by Stephanie Spinner & Jonathan Etra
Julian books by Ann Cameron
The Katie Lynn Cookie Company series
  by G. E. Stanley
The Case of the Elevator Duck
  by Polly Berrien Berends
Hannah by Gloria Whelan
Little Swan by Adèle Geras
The Minstrel in the Tower
  by Gloria Skurzynski

Next Spring an Oriole
  by Gloria Whelan
Night of the Full Moon
  by Gloria Whelan
Silver by Gloria Whelan
Smasher by Dick King-Smith

CLASSICS
Dr. Jekyll and Mr. Hyde
  retold by Stephanie Spinner
Dracula retold by Stephanie Spinner
Frankenstein retold by Larry Weinbe**

Grades 3–5

FICTION
The Magic Elements Quartet
  by Mallory Loehr
Spider Kane Mysteries
  by Mary Pope Osborne

NONFICTION
Balto and the Great Race
  by Elizabeth Cody Kimmel
The *Titanic* Sinks!
  by Thomas Conklin